REMAINS

LEE GARRATT

ISBN: 978-1-989940-22-8
Copyright © 2021 Lee Garratt
Dimensionfold Publishing
Prince George BC CAN

Contents

1.

The land stretched in all directions as far as the boy could see. To the north, a plain of dust and rubbish. It was usually hazy with grit whipped up by the wind that always seemed to blow, but, on the rare occasions the wind dropped and the view cleared, the boy scoured the infinite distances for the horseback raiders he had heard tales about all his life. To the south, it was more undulating, with small hummocks starting almost from the foot of the small village. Upon the top of one of these, a faint green smudge could be seen by those with the keenest eyes. That, the boy was told, was the forest. The boy tried and failed to imagine the sickly, yellowing growths that sometimes struggled through the mud by the creek, towering and crowding around him, full of life.

From west to east, the small creek ran. It seemed no larger downstream than up, no vigorous upstream than down. It ran its sinuous, lazy course without hope. Rebecca told him that it would, eventually, reach the sea. Alfred turned away from the promise of that word as if the salt stung his eyes.

The village hardly deserved the name. A handful of buildings in various states of disrepair that threatened to fall down, and sometimes did, whenever the storms blew. Alfred lived in the grandest of the surviving houses, such as that was. His family had run the inn for as far back as anyone could remember. The travellers' route was little used now. Sometimes three or four days would pass with no one coming through. But, from time to time, a man would appear out of the wastes, slowly drawing closer, occasionally bending to the ground, inspecting something, then placing it in the sack they always carried. When they arrived, they were happy to eat and drink the meagre food the inn could provide, happily handing over barter or even that rarest of things, coin.

The village owed its reason for being to these travellers and, as they had grown fewer, so the settlement had shrunk. The remains of abandoned buildings surrounded what few survived. Alfred's main chore was to raise crops from the poor land that surrounded them. Rain was seldom, but the main problem was the land itself. Poisoned, some said. Cursed, others. No matter how often Alfred picked out and threw away the metal and plastic rubbish that was everywhere, the next day there was more. Shards of metal poking through the soil where green shoots should be, bowls of plastic bulging where turnips should be blooming, purple with life. "If we could eat this shit, we'd all be fat as kings", he remembered his father once said in one of his few attempts at humour. It did seem a miracle to Alfred.

Where did it all come from? No one knew. He was one of those in the village who thought these manifestations of rubbish were the excrescences of a diseased earth. Like the blood clots, he saw people coughing up. Or scabs. The land was sick, he thought.

He had been in their plot hacking at the ground when his father had shouted for him. Alfred was shocked that he hadn't heard or seen the traveller's approach. He had a skill for this and took some pride in it. That the traveller must have come from the north was apparent – all the plots were on the south side to take what little shelter they could from the dust storms. This made him of more interest to Alfred; travellers seldom came from that direction these days.

He was already settled when Alfred bustled into the cool and shade. Browned by the weather, he was sat, the sack of his hoard by his side, and there, fussing on his lap, was a puppy. Alfred was transfixed; he had never seen one before. No dogs lived in sight of the village. The villagers would kill and eat them if they could. Alfred had occasionally heard them howling in the distance on cold, winter nights.

The man looked up and saw the boy looking. He smiled, blue eyes and white teeth cracking the dark grime of his face. "Come here lad," he said and beckoned him over. "Here". He passed the bundle to him, Alfred holding his breath. It was blind still. It sucked onto his fingers and mewed. "Found it", the man went on, "by his mum. She'd died along with his brothers and sisters. Just hunger, I think. They are very rare now these."

Alfred felt a shadow fall on him; his father was stood glaring down at him. The traveller retrieved the puppy. "Go on lad now, help your dad". Alfred hurried off, feeling the heat of his father's displeasure on him.

The boy lingered near throughout the rest of the man's stay, took away his dishes, cleaned his table. The puppy had fallen asleep after being given some food from the man's plate. The man had then taken out a book and a pencil from somewhere on his person and had started making some notes in it. His father grabbed his arm as he sallied off on another needless cleaning trip. "That's enough now", he hissed. "That man's trouble". His father glared at him over his black beard. "Leave him be".

The boy had never seen anyone write in a book before. His mother had had a book for him from somewhere as a child. He vaguely remembered being shown pages with a dragon and a picture of a castle turret with pink roses growing near it. His mother could read, and Alfred had learnt the alphabet from his mother, always with his father clattering nearby, scowling in disapproval at such a wasteful use of the boy's time. But write in a book? No. The boy was always intrigued by travellers, piecing together their imagined lives, but never had his interest been piqued like this before. The man was similar to others who had passed through but, somehow, of a different quality. His face was nut brown and lined from the sun, but he handled a pen dexterously. He was wrapped in the loose robes that most travellers favoured, but his, while still plain and homespun, seemed of a better, thicker material.

The man didn't rush but, after the heat of the midday had started to pass, he began to gather himself. He won over his father a little by paying with real silver coin. It was far too much really, as the man would have noticed if he had seen how his father clasped on to it. Maybe he didn't care, thought Alfred. And he wondered again about the muck they hauled from the ground.

The man thanked the man for the meal and, gathering his belongings, left. Making an excuse of taking some rubbish out, Alfred found the man just outside, looking at the contents of his sack. The man gave him a sly grin. "Come here lad. You know this is what we collect right?"

Alfred did know it, remembering the shock and disappointment the first time he had seen a traveller's 'treasure'. He had imagined something precious like the gold or diamonds or rubies he remembered from his mother's books. So, when Alfred had seen the sack open to show the metal and plastic that cursed all the land around here, that was so abundant that he never stopped pulling it from the ground, he had thought at first he had been taken as a fool in some elaborate joke. Since then, he had cast this disappointment from his mind and, strangely he now reflected, never really thought of it again; just put it down as another eccentricity of these strange travellers that no sensible folk could reckon with.

Now though, as he looked again, he noticed that he had only been half correct. Metal and plastic waste yes, but it was of a quality and kind that showed a man had sought for it, not just randomly picked up. The metal was of different types, uncorroded and in regular shapes. The plastic was shaped and whole, not malformed. "You are puzzled by this, aren't you?" The boy looked up at him. "What do you know of it?". The boy was taken aback. To be asked his opinion was a novel experience. "Well ....it comes from the ground. All around here", he began haltingly.

"Go on", the man encouraged.

"That some think it was made by man. Others that it springs from the ground like a sickness". The man looked at him appraisingly. His eyes were as blue as a cold winter's sky. "And what is it that you think Alfred?" The boy was struck again- the man had taken note of his name! Alfred went to talk of his theory, that these protuberances were like the boils or the tumours that burst forth from the villager's bodies. But something stopped him. Instead, he spoke a thought that until now had never occurred to him.

"I think that man made this. Somehow. A long time ago".

The man laughed and clapped him on the back. "Ha. Yes, and that's about the sum of it. Not many know much more. Maybe some of the masters in Seacity. Yes, man made these once." The man ran his fingers through them, making a clatter. "And ruined everything somehow with it too."

"Why do you say that," the boy asked. The man looked around as if taking in the village, lost in the wastes, for the first time.

"I don't think it should come naturally from the ground like this boy. It doesn't grow. And us," he beckoned with his arm, "I don't think we always lived.....like this. All our places were much bigger once, grander." He started to haul his sack onto the cart, tied it on securely. He turned again to the boy. "You're a good lad, I can tell. You know, there is more to the world, even now, than this. A few hovels in the dirt". He spat on the floor. "Seacity boy. That's a place where some of the learning still persists. You should go there one day." The man looked at him searchingly. Something going on behind his eyes, judgements being weighed and discounted until, finally, with a sigh, he decided. He shuffled in his robes for something, then held it out. Alfred took it. A red plastic object. Small. Roundish. Warm on his palm. On it the figure of a man hauling a sack on the top. Alfred turned it over. A soaring turret with the rooves of buildings going into the distance. "Keep that. You should come to Seacity. There we are can always use intelligent people.

And the world is starting to change again. You'll see. Keep it, and if you ever make it, you should ask for me, Harald, and show that. It's my mark. A token, we call it. If I'm still around, I might make use of you. Now, I'd best get going Alfred. The road is a long one."

As he took up the rope for the mule, the puppy started to wriggle again. "Ah, no you don't", the man grabbed it with one hand, stopped it spilling to the ground. Then he stopped and turned again to look at the boy, mulling something over. "Here," he said, offering the boy the puppy. The boy stood stunned. This was beyond what he had imagined. A puppy. His own puppy. "Here", the man laughed, proffering it again. "It will be too much of a nuisance for me on the road, I think. And it will be hard for me to look after it". The boy stretched out his arms and took it into his arms. Warm and wriggling and biting. "It will be hard for you to look after too, I think, but not too hard. These dogs can live on almost nothing. They'll eat anything you have. And, when it is a little bit older, I reckon it will catch most of what you need. There'll be some crabs down there, I reckon?" The man nodded to the river.

"Yes", the boy said.

"Well, he'll dig them out alright. He'll make a fine pet for a boy such as you, I think. See you, Alfred". And with that, the man took his mule and set off. Alfred watched, but the rolling small hills and dunes soon swallowed up the traveller.

The boy fussed with the puppy, finding it some bones from the rubbish that it cheerfully crunched up. "Harald", he whispered. "I'll call you Harald after that nice man".

"You'll look after that and feed it all by yourself", his father's voice broke in. The boy turned around, holding Harald into his chest. His father stood there in the shadow of the open doorway looking at him, disapprovingly as always. How long had he been stood there watching him? "You will not feed it any of our food. You understand that, don't you Alfred". The boy nodded. "Make sure of it", his father went on. "Now, come on, help me in here". Alfred walked over, holding the token in his pocket as he did so.

x

The traveller was right. Harald was easy to look after even though his father initially refused to let it live in the hut. However, despite the initial curses and throwing anything that

5

came to hand when Harald came skulking in, his father's rule quickly subsided into muttered cursing as he sat in the evening, endlessly drinking the weak beer he favoured. So, Harald quickly had the run of the place, sleeping with Alfred in the night.

Alfred loved his company, and on cold nights, or when the wind really blew, enjoyed the warmth. Alfred was quick to clean up any mess Harald made, fearing the wrath of his father, but that didn't last long. Harald conveniently favoured an out of the way spot behind the hut. There was never much food thrown away. He and his father and most travellers were always hungry and consumed most meals in silence, with an urgency. But there was some. Spoiled meat. Stale bread. Bones. These Alfred always gave to the dog, which it took without any fuss. And Harald was a quick learner.

A month or two passed, and Alfred was stooped over on the garden worrying at the ground, pulling at the endless garbage whilst sowing a new crop of turnips, when he noticed that Harald, rather than walking around him snapping at the flies, or lying down basking in the sun, had disappeared. Intrigued, the boy started to scout around for him, calling him. As he circled the house, he heard a scurry of pebbles, a quick yap and a scream. Rounding the building, he saw Harald trotting towards him with a fat bloody rat in his mouth. He seemed very pleased with himself, as was Alfred until Harald started to consume the still living creature in front of him.

From then on, Harald was largely self-sufficient, and a varied array of creatures remains were soon being shovelled into the soil as food for the crops. Alfred was surprised at the number of animals Harald was able to find. Rats were his main food source and, when Alfred pointed that out to his father, that earned what could have been a grunt of approval. But there were other things too. Lizards, some of a size Alfred had never seen before. Burrowing creatures, with large shovel hands and smooth blind faces. Alfred assumed Harald had taken these a little away from the village for all of the villagers would take and eat these animals too, given half a chance.

Some things Alfred had never seen before. Spiny things. Leathery things. Things with dark wet faces filled with shiny teeth that Alfred thought Harald had taken from the creek. He wondered then why dogs didn't live closer to the village if there was enough food to eat. Perhaps, he surmised, if there were many more than just one dog, there quickly wouldn't be enough.

And when Alfred saw some of the hungry glances some of the villagers cast towards Harald, it gave him another, more unpleasant, thought. Such thoughts meant Alfred was as vigilant as he could be to Harald's presence, but he assumed that his father's reputation would dissuade others, no matter how hungry they were. His father might not like the dog, but he wouldn't brook any villager being bold enough to make such an assault on his authority.

Alfred's disgust at the thoughts some of the villagers harboured for his pet were mingled with pity. He was forever unsure how some of them survived. A rough form of barter existed in the village. Eyful, made the beer his dad always drank. Arnald, a rough kind of flour. All had a garden of some sort, most lay traps for the same creatures that Harald took. (Alfred and his father were above such things). But most of the villagers were sickening in some way. Their gardens were ill-kept, the bread poorly made. Most just seemed to spend their days lying on their beds or sat outside in the sun. They hardly even collected together, few in numbers as they were, preferring their own company even though their neighbour might only be within spitting distance. I suppose, thought Alfred, they weren't really living anymore, just slowly dying. What he was seeing was the last, drawn out, dying breath of the village.

There was only one other child in the village, Rebecca. Her parents were both sick and wasted, with barely the energy to get out of bed. Rebecca did everything; kept the garden, milked the animals, cooked and cleaned. She never complained though, and, on the days she was kept too busy to speak to Alfred in person, would always wave when she saw him. Alfred thought once what would he do with himself if Rebecca had not been around, if he was the only child left. He quickly turned away from that thought as too horrible to contemplate, imagining himself alone with the others in the village. He remembered old John, who he had last seen crawling across the ground towards the river.

Alfred had come on him one morning. He had thought, for one shocking moment, that someone lay dead till he saw a sudden, scrabbling movement with the arms and a pathetic kicking of the legs. "Where are you going, John? Are you okay?" he had asked uselessly. Old John had murmured something then, in a voice wracked with pain. He had been in pain for a long time, Alfred knew. Like most in the village, his limbs had never been true, suffering from the strange growths that seemed to plague the villagers, always bubbling and boiling up through the skin. John had had it worse than most, and he had heard him, cursing and groaning on quiet nights. His father had appeared then and pulled John back to his house, the wrecked man moaning all the way. "Want to drown", Alfred heard him say, "lemme drown". Alfred recoiled from the pained man dragging himself over to the shallow muddy river, barely deep enough for the job.

Alfred never saw John again, and now his house lay empty and in a state of increasing disrepair. There was no grave for him. Alfred tried not to think about what had happened.

Only Rebecca lay between him and the unrelenting nature of this misery and pain and cruelty. He had known her for as long as he could remember, and they had always been friends. They had never fallen out - it just didn't seem something that could happen. When they were small, they had made clay figures and played with them for hours in the scanty yellow grass. For years, they had played this game, the lives of these make-believe villagers becoming so real to him that he remembered becoming tearful when one of them broke during their play.

Rebecca loved Harald as he did. Even though the villagers frowned upon their antics, and his father barked at him to 'stay close, Harald's natural inquisitiveness gave them even more excuse to wander further afield. One day Rebecca had appeared at his garden unannounced. Alfred hadn't even heard her arrive, bent over, sweating, pulling up the weed that seemed to love the soil almost as much as the rubbish did. He heard a scuffling behind him and turned around to see Rebecca tumbling with Harald on the floor, the dog nipping and biting at her as she laughed. "What are you doing here," Alfred asked. Rebecca didn't normally arrive like this, kept busy with chores he normally had to find her out. "Ah", she said, looking at the floor, "they're tired today. Sleeping."

Alfred thought they must be finally dying, but he had felt that for a long time and somehow, they seemed to persist. Like the yarrow weed. Or the rubbish. He felt guilty for thinking that. Maybe they had been nice people once when they weren't old and in pain. All they did now were fester and stink in the dark. It would be a relief for Rebecca if they died, he thought. He never told her that.

"Come on", she said. "Let's go". They set off in their usual direction, around the house, keeping away from the open front door where his father would probably shout at them, out into the low hillocks that stretched to the south. They were as about as lush as they ever got, with the yellowing grass thickening to the children's knees. The odd low tree could be spotted here and there, with little green leaves starting to jut out. Harald scampered around, snapping at the insects that buzzed just out of his reach. Rebecca limped alongside him, both children content to walk. "I don't think they were always like they are now, you know", she said. Perhaps because they spent so much time together, they had started to hear each other's thoughts. "They must have been children once. Like us. It's the pain, I think. Being in pain for years and years".

"Are you in pain", Alfred asked immediately regretting it.

"Yes." She replied. "But it's ok. I'm young." She smiled. "You're not in pain, are you?" she asked.

"No. I don't think so anyway." They both laughed at this stupid response. There was then a sudden flurry of activity. Harald bolted past them, the grass bending and furrowing just ahead of him, where a blur of black could just be seen. Whatever it was, made it to some rocks, where Harald ran around madly before squeezing behind one and disappearing.

The children ran, Alfred arriving first as usual. He rolled the boulder out of the way to uncover a small hole that went into the hill. There were some droppings at the entrance. There weren't many animals he thought it could be. Something of that size, he could only think of a large rat, but it didn't seem to move quite the same.

He bent to the hole. He couldn't see or hear anything. "Harald", he shouted. Nothing. Rebecca arrived, grimacing slightly with the sudden activity. "He's in there", she indicated. Alfred nodded. "He'll work his way out," she said. "He's a clever dog".

Where Harald went to over the next few hours was forever a mystery to Alfred. He couldn't imagine the creature, whatever it was, had created too extensive a labyrinth of tunnels. They both shouted and even tried excavating into the side of the hill to expose the tunnels, but it was hopeless. The ground was too hard, and they didn't have any tools. All they achieved were skinned knuckles. Hours had passed, and they were both sat slumped on the hill, unwilling to accept Harald's loss. Tears streaked Rebecca's face. Alfred couldn't bear to think of Harald stuck in there but, like a scab that he knew he shouldn't pick, he kept returning to the image. Harald squirming, stuck in the blackness. Then, suddenly, they heard a scrabbling that got closer, and he trotted out, muddied, tongue lolling, as if he hadn't been gone more than a few moments. They fell on him, amazed.

The sun was setting now, and they had a little way to walk home, out of sight beyond the slight rise. This was something of a taboo. No one ventured out far after dark. In the evenings, sometimes Alfred would gaze out at the profound blackness. On moonless, cloudy nights, the black was so immense and dark that he felt dizzy. This evening though, the sky was clear, the first stars already twinkled overhead and, despite their transgression, with Harald newly with them again, the children were joyous.

The sky quickly darkened as they went up a slight rise and, broaching the top, they saw their village, in a different direction than they had thought it, and further away. Alfred shivered a little at the thought of them getting lost out here. There was no real danger, he supposed, in this immensity of dark, the village's fires would be visible for many miles away. He noticed though, that Rebecca had been labouring more than usual up the slight hill. "Come on, let's have a little sit-down. It's night when we get back now, no matter how we rush." There was a small tree there, and Alfred fancied he had noticed this small hill before from his home. They sat for a while, looking at the village. "My father will be angry," Alfred said.

"Oh, he's always angry", Rebecca replied.

"Ah yes, but this time he will be really angry. I've never been out at night before. He'll beat me for this." Rebecca didn't say anything. There was nothing to say. They both looked at the immensity of the sky. The stars were incredible. Alfred thrilled and shrank from their cold distance. Then, at the same moment, they both noticed a different light, closer, more rounded, orange, floating lower to the horizon. "There," they both said.

Alfred had seen one of these before. Some years ago. He had asked his father what it was. "Eyes, watching us", he had growled.

Alfred told Rebecca this, "What is it do you think?" he asked.

"I remember that. My parents said the same. The next day, I asked again, and they said it was from the Seacity. They travelled by balloon to keep an eye on their distant lands".

"Do they own us?" Alfred said. He had heard of the Seacity, of course. All the travellers seemed to be going or leaving from there. And occasionally, they would say a few things about it. A city, many houses all together, markets full of food. Towers. Books. Alfred often thought of it. He struggled to picture it as a real place that actually existed.

"I think so", Rebecca said. "Though I don't think they could be particularly interested in us. What could we give them?" she laughed.

"But why do they travel at night? They can't exactly see much."

"I don't know. Maybe it's just chance. They come up very rarely, I think. Maybe just passing through these lands as not much of interest."

They sat a little while longer as the night cooled around them. Alfred produced the token Harald had given him, dark under the moonlight. Rebecca looked at it wonderingly, both exclaiming at the size of the city, Seacity surely, an expanse of rooves stretching off from a turret. They tried and failed to imagine the sandy wastes around them full of buildings and people as far as they could see.

Eventually, they picked themselves up and set off towards the lights. With each step closer, Alfred grew more nervous. They whispered goodbye at the outskirts of the village, then Alfred tried to sneak his way inside. His father was sat there. A large jug of half-drunk beer sat next to him. A bowl of something brown steaming before him.

"Where've you been," he said, barely looking up.

"Just with Rebecca. In her house," he blurted out weakly, regretting these words as soon as he had said them.

"Liar", his father said in a calm voice. "I've been there. You haven't". Alfred said nothing. The calmness of his father unnerved him. "It's that bloody dog, isn't it".

Alfred started to protest. "No, it's...." but was interrupted.

"It bloody is. Don't argue with me." His father's voice was raised now, looking up at Alfred with black eyes. "You know you are not to go out at night, don't you. You know that?".

"Yes, sorry", Alfred mumbled. "We didn't go far we....."

"Shut up", his father broke in. "You are not to go out of the village at night."

"But why" he replied weakly.

"Why?" his father exploded. "Why? Because it's dangerous. Snakes that poison you. Other beasts. There are hardly any of us as it is. If you died, or Rebecca, that's the end of this village". Alfred could hardly remember his father speaking such a long sentence before. He had never thought of this. It suddenly struck him that he and Rebecca were precious, seen as such. They were the last chance for this dying place. His father's words tailed off, and he reverted again to eating his stew. Alfred slunk off and fell into a sleep filled with strange, vivid dreams of balloons and strangers.

When he awoke the following day, he could tell by the light that he had slept in late. It was quiet, he thought, then realised he was alone. Harald wasn't curled up with him as usual. Curious, he rose and dressed. Alfred could tell by the silence that his father wasn't there. He walked outside. Though the sun was behind a high veil of cloud, it was bright, with an oppressive flat white glare. He couldn't see his father at first, then looking around slightly, he noticed him not far to the north, hunched over something in the waste. He felt a sickness in his stomach as he walked quickly before breaking into a run.

His father was hunched over a small pit and, as he watched, he saw him throw the small, broken body into it. His father had heard him then and turned around. He stood up. "I told you about this bloody dog..."

Alfred looked down at Harald. He seemed smaller in the hole. A thin covering of soil covered his flank. His vision blurred. "I don't care what you fucking said. You're a fucking bastard. I fucking hate you. Harald hadn't done anything to you." He stood there shaking with rage, sick at the loss. And as he stood there, he could feel the eyes of the village on him. Voices of any kind were rare enough. It seemed people were almost scared to break the pall of silence that lay on the village. But raised voices were very unusual.

His father looked at him. His brow furrowed. "Careful now, Alfred," he said in a low voice.

"Ah fuck off. You're horrible. A fucking bastard". Alfred had never said anything like this before. He felt a sudden rush of freedom before his father strode over to him and, grabbing him by the collar, hauled him off. His father was strong and took him with no effort, dragged him into the centre of the village, then threw him on the ground.

The villagers were all out now. Impassive but curious faces, looking on. 'Where was Rebecca' Alfred thought, oddly calm.

"I've been too soft with you. I can see that now", his father was saying. "I only did that because of her...." ('her', Alfred thought, 'his mum?') "...but that's the end. There are rules. You will follow them." His father hit him then right in the face. Strangely it didn't seem to hurt, but he could taste the iron tang of blood. He fell to the floor. His father started to kick him then, shouting words at him he couldn't hear. Alfred thought then of his mum for the first time in years. He suddenly remembered her in the garden, her seeing him and her face breaking into a smile as he tottered towards her, her picking him up and hugging him, blonde, blue eyes.

The blows stopped then. A confusion of voices. Hands picking him up. A man stood there he had never seen before. Dark skinned. He was wearing a rough, cloth smock bound at the waist by a belt of some sort. "You're ok now," he said, looking at him. He heard an argument behind him and turned around. A small woman in the same uniform stood there. She wore something strange on her eyes. She was talking to her father. He could see Rebecca now, mouthing at him, "are you alright?". His father was shouting. "He is my son. How dare you. Who the fuck are you?".

"I am Morgeth Traborne. Myself and Garth here", she indicated the tall, dark man who had picked Alfred up, "are empowered by the council at Seacity to undertake a census of this part of our lands. We are also", she produced then a scroll from her garments, "by the powers invested here, given protection and some basic powers. We do have the powers of arrest Mr.......".

"John", his father replied. "Well, that's as maybe", he continued in a lower voice, "but I still don't see what I was doing wrong. Are fathers not allowed to discipline their sons in Seacity?"

"They are allowed to discipline, of course, but physically beat them senseless in the public road? No, that will not do." A silence fell then. His father, Alfred could see, was humiliated. He had never known anyone to talk to him like this.

"I see", he went on. "Well, you are a long way from home doing this important work. I imagine any kind of accident could befall people such as you on such a job?". His dark eyes glittered dangerously.

"That is true", the woman said. "And that is why there are always two of us. And… "she eyed here his fathers bunched fists, "it would be most unfortunate if any 'accident' befell us now. Not two days have passed since we sent message that this", she signalled around at the village, "would be our next visit. You can be reassured that any such 'accident' that might befall us would be duly investigated by more of us than you see here. Guards too, probably." He could see his father come to a decision. "Well," he said. "I suppose you must be staying here. You can fucking have him tonight". He glared at Alfred and strode off as Alfred sunk to the floor again, darkness overtaking him.

2.

When he woke, he was in a canvas tent. There was a cool breeze, and the sun fell in across his body. It was pleasant to lie there and feel the breeze. When he moved his body, he could feel the soreness. He lay there for some while before he heard steps and voices coming closer. A woman and man approached and knelt in at the doorway. "Hello", the woman said. "You're up".

"Yes. What ....."

"Don't worry. We thought it best to look after you since that... unfortunate incident. You took a beating, but you are okay, we think." The man returned then with a mug of some drink, a herbal tea of some kind. "Drink," she said, "this'll do you good".

Alfred drank it. It was very bitter.

"We have some work to do", she said. "We can talk later. Don't worry." She smiled then and walked away.

The next couple of days were very odd. The strangers had camped a short distance away from the village but close enough that, when Alfred looked, he could see his father busying himself around the house. The census takers, as they called themselves, busied themselves around the village. He watched them walking around, talking to the villagers, taking notes. When they returned to the camp on the first night, Garth showed him their books. There were more numbers than he had expected. He asked them what they were doing. "It is a simple job in many ways," Garth said, a smile creasing his face, "we are here just to record. How many people live here is the main thing, I suppose, but also their ages, health, sex, how people live and so on. It is all here. We call it a census". The man smiled.

"Why?" Alfred asked.

"Seacity wants to know. All these lands are part of Seacity really, even here. You are about the furthest away of all the settlements, so it is a long time that there were any meaningful links. There were a lot more in the past, but it all fell away with the raids. Then the wars. But now, things are starting to improve. Seacity is growing again, reaching out. This visit is the first step in that."

They only stayed for one more day, Alfred spending much of that fussing and wondering over the horse. Jasper, Garth called it. Brown all over except for its fetlocks, all of which were white. Such a beast had seemed impossible to him when he had heard them described, but seeing it now, he wondered at his previous incredulity; it seemed harder now to imagine a world without one. Stood there, stroking it, feeding it with the best food he could find, Alfred had started to harbour hopes that they would take him with them. There was nothing for him here – only Rebecca. The woman must have guessed that, for on the second night, while they were eating the dried meat and fruits they carried with them, she said, "We can't take you, you know Alfred. We would do, you know. We've even asked your father, but he wouldn't agree to it."

"I don't care. You could just take me. I want to go with you."

"I would like to, Alfred. Even though that would complicate things slightly, and I would be asked many difficult questions on my return", she smiled. "But I can't. You are too young to make your own decisions. And he is your father. We are given a variety of powers with our role, but none of them includes breaking the laws of the land." She sensed the boy's disappointment. "Hey", she said, touching him. Her face was close to him, the glasses that she wore and had explained to him how they worked, magnifying her eyes slightly. He looked at them now, bright and brown. "Don't worry too much. I do not doubt that the next few years will be tough. But you're a tough kid." She punched him. "I have explained exactly to your dad the fulsome nature of our report here. I have also explained to him that we have recorded everything we have observed and witnessed, including this", she motioned to one of Alf's bruises, "….our full report on everyone who lives here including you", she pointed at his chest."…And how on our next visit we will be fully expecting everyone to be in good health or there will be consequences." She paused. "You will be safe", she said in a quieter voice. "And I'm sorry to hear about Harald. That was a very cruel thing to have done."

"How?" the boy whispered. The woman looked out for a moment before replying. "We have spoken to Rebecca amongst all the other villagers ". There were a few moments of silence then. Alfred didn't know what to say; having a conversation with someone other than Rebecca felt very odd.

"You'll be back?" he eventually muttered.

"Yes", she replied. "This is the first step really on re-establishing ties and links. Going forwards there will be more visits of different kinds. Doctors. Teachers".

"Will you come back?" the boy said.

"Perhaps", she smiled. "Perhaps I will. In which case you should know my name. I'm Martha."

On the morning of the first day, they left, loading up Jasper with their possessions, munching quite contentedly on the weeds and garden refuse while they busied around him. They walked over to his father's house, where his father was ostentatiously trying to ignore them, preparing some meal for a traveller sat in the shade. Alfred was amazed to realise he had never even noticed him arrive. The woman coughed. "Here is Alfred, as discussed." She had her hand on his shoulder. "You'll remember what we said." His father's eyes raised slightly in acknowledgement. There was no more of a goodbye than that. She held his shoulder then they both said goodbye. And that was that. He watched them walk off, following the river, slowly disappearing in the haze.

X

The woman was right. The following year or so was tough but, in truth, no more than it had always been. His father was perhaps more taciturn than usual, but there weren't any more beatings. His father's interest in him seemed to have shrunk, and Alfred came to realise that with that came an increased freedom. He no longer seemed to care what Alfred did or where he wandered. Not that there were many places to go, but just knowing that he could, if he wanted, just wander off, set off to Seacity filled the boy with hope.

One day he was down at the creek with Rebecca. If it weren't for this tiny river, the little life in the village would quickly shrivel to nothing. Most of the villager's food came from the fish and crabs they could get here. It was only small, but there were only a few villagers, most of whom hardly seemed to eat anymore. The villagers had set up some simple traps years ago slightly upstream and, though some weeks these were empty, most of the time they contained at least a few meals. The crabs fascinated Alfred. They were wary and hard to find. They burrowed into the mud banks and, on hot days, couldn't be found. The time to look for them was when the sun was going down or on cooler days when clouds blew in from the east. Where the sea lay, they said, an unthinkable distance away. This was one of those days, and he and Rebecca were down at their usual crab hunting spot. She was sat on the dry bank laughing at

17

him, floundering bare-legged in the mud. "You won't find them", she laughed. "They're too quick for you", as she said that though, in perfect timing, one suddenly scuttled out from behind a large lump of metal Alfred had dislodged. He jumped on it quickly, hoisting it in triumph above him. It was a large one.
A short while later, after they had made a quick low fire and boiled it up, they were sat there happily, still licking their fingers.

"You know, why don't we just go," Alfred said.
"Go", she said. "Where?".
"To Seacity".
Rebecca laughed. "You're mad".
"Why am I? People do it all the time. Travellers. The census takers."
"Yes, but they know what they're doing. They know where they're going. They have provisions."
"They don't have much," Alfred said, which was true. Most of the travellers didn't seem to have much apart from the rubbish they trawled from the ground. "There must be a place they go. We could just follow them. It would be easy. No one would even think that was what we were doing. We could just walk out of here. "
Rebecca sat and thought, and suddenly the total simplicity of it hit her. Alfred too, his own words had seemed to breathe life into an idea he hadn't even thought of a few minutes ago. They both laughed. "Yes," she said. "We could, I suppose." She paused. "But I can't yet". Alfred knew why. Even though her father had passed last year, a blessing, the end just a stinking death, her mother still clung on. "But, yes, ok. We will". She looked up at him then and smiled, and Alfred, in that moment, experienced a feeling new to him – hope.

x

Around a year after the visit of the Seacity, a traveller arrived from the north. Although this was still far from usual (most came from other compass points, arriving at their village as their very furthest destination before starting their journey back towards the Seacity), such visits from the north had become more numerous in recent months. Travellers were often not the most talkative of guests but most now seemed a little more at ease in themselves. "Business is good", Alfred had heard one say. "Seacity is reaching out, you'll see", another had

18

said, smiling to him before handing over an actual coin in payment. He had turned it over in his hand. A crown on an anchor, the sign of the city. He had kept this by his bed and looked at it most nights.

This traveller though, huddled grimly in the shadows of the corner of the pub, the reflections of the firelight playing dully in a silver buckle that clasped his belt together. His face looked pained and tired beneath the grime of his journey. Alfred tried to engage him. He didn't seem short of coin and, after a large meal of vegetables and fish, looked up at him.

"You should leave here lad", he muttered. Alfred looked up, startled slightly by this sudden bald statement.

"Why?" Alfred said.

"You aren't the only village up here, you know. There are one or two more. One is so far up to the wastelands that many of the occupants are raiders themselves, or were once before they settled down. Anyway, I am told, by others who have heard I don't know how, that that village has gone now."

"Gone", Alfred repeated stupidly.

"Aye gone lad. Gone from the face of the earth. Everyone dead or carried off. The raiders lad. They're moving again."

Alfred felt a roiling in his stomach. He couldn't help take a look to the north as he did so.

"I don't know how long it will be before they're here lad. Maybe tomorrow. Maybe never. But if they're on the move, I'm away from there, and so is every traveller. I'll be telling the Seacity when I get there."

Alfred thought on the man's words. Said them to Rebecca. He even mentioned it to his father, who grunted that the traveller was "probably mad" and carried on with what he was doing. He even thought of heading off as the man had suggested. But that day didn't seem the right day. The sun was shining, and he had a full belly. And the north looked much the same as it always had. So the days went on as before. The traveller they decided was exaggerating. Raiders were from the old times. Maybe they were getting stronger again but raiding? This far south? And anyway, the Seacity would be reaching out soon, wouldn't it? On a sunny day, lying down by the creek, they dismissed it. It seemed impossible, lying here, feet in the river.

"Probably been out too long in the sun", Rebecca ventured. "All of them are half crazy anyway".

Alfred thought of Harald and disagreed, but she was mostly right. They turned again to the subject they had been skirting around for months, ever since the visitors. "So, when are we going to leave Rebecca".

She dug in the mud with her toe. "I'm not going to leave with mother still alive," she said. "I don't think that will be too long though", she went on, looking down at her feet.

"Is she bad?" Alfred said. He hadn't properly seen her in years, just glimpses of her lying down in the gloom or tottering, weakly, about.

"Yes. She hardly moves now. Hardly eats. Drinks." She shook her head. "It won't be long."

"Well, we can wait for the visitors to return anyway. I'll be full grown soon. You are already. If they come after then, and your mum has….gone, we could just go with them."

"Yes, we could," Rebecca added. "Seacity might be coming out here, but I think they'll be too late. This place is nearly dead."

A month later, on a day of rare dank drizzle from high grey clouds, Rebecca's mother died. Rebecca had come to him to ask for help, and, of course, he had, though, as he walked to her place, he felt an increasing sense of dread. The house was so dark, with patched up curtains on the window, that, as he entered, he found it difficult to see anything in the gloom. He watched Rebecca go over to the corner of the room, and then he saw her, skin withered to the bone, mouth agape. The sweet stink of death came off her making him gag. Rebecca had already dressed and washed her so there wasn't much to do. "What do you want to do, Rebecca?"

"Oh, let's just bury her," she said, looking down at her mother. "Noone cares about her apart from me. Noone ever visited."

The last time one of the villagers died, Shebbel, two years ago, there had been a funeral where all the villagers had gathered as they always had. But even since then, life in the village had decreased even further. Barely anyone socialised anymore. Most were decrepit. Alfred's father was easily the strongest and most vital of those who remained. The travellers that visited Alfred's home sheltered him a little from this stark and obvious realisation. There wasn't a village anymore, just four old and sickly people, his father, himself and Rebecca. They wrapped her in the sheet and carried her out.

"Where do you want to go," Alfred asked.

"The garden", Rebecca replied. "I can remember her in there when I was a little girl. She liked it once, I remember. And it would be nice, I think. For her to give life again."

So they dug a hole there, not as deep as maybe it should have been, but the ground was hard and the day hot, and placed her in. Alfred stood up, sweating from his exertions. He looked around at the nearby houses. If anyone had been watching, they weren't now. Silence.

They didn't say anything. Just placed her there and stood for a moment before covering her with soil.

The visitors returned the next day. Alfred heard them singing before he saw them. Song! He ran out of his house, and there they were cresting a low rise to the south. Five of them and two horses, the flash of white on one of them must be Jasper, Garth, tall and dark-skinned next to him. And there, in the middle, the shortest of the group, Martha. She saw him and waved.

X

There had never been activity in the village like this before. This time they came into the settlement and quickly occupied two of the houses that were still standing. They then set to work. Garth conducted medical checks on everyone, his open smile seeming to bring a warmth into the villagers' houses that had been missing for a long time. He looked in Alfred's mouth, in his ears, listened to his chest. He stood up and grinned. "A bit skinny, but you're fit! I won't waste any more time on you." He then went over to help one of his colleagues with Eyful, who seemed to be needing more attention.

Others started to busy themselves around the gardens of the village. Alfred helped Martha with this, showing them how they farmed the land, what they grew. They seemed interested and asked more questions scribbling all the time in their books. They then went down to the fish traps and, at Alfred's insistence, to the mud banks to see the crabs.

Two days later, they had what they called a 'party'. It was supposedly being held to celebrate Garth heading back to Seacity, he had messages to take they said, but Alfred and Rebecca thought that just a convenient excuse. A fire was built, they produced meat which they roasted, and, all the time, Garth played on his musical instrument and sang, with the others joining in on particular favourites. Rebecca was there, of course, and one of the women with the group started to show her dance steps to one of their songs, hauling Alfred to his feet too. They stepped in time to the music, clapping their hands together before turning about. To Alfred's great surprise, his father had been there too. Alfred was amazed to see him crack a smile, and even more so when he got on to his feet and hobbled in time to the rhythm. Alfred felt a wave of guilt. He had come to see the villagers as all strangely hating him for some reason, but, perhaps, he too was guilty of what had happened. Maybe they all were. He thought back to years ago, and he could remember times when his father had spoken to him more often, with more warmth. Perhaps he was as guilty as the others of the silence that had fallen on them.

Later, when the music fell softer, Alfred and Rebecca spoke to Martha. Rebecca surprised him in talking first. "We want to come with you when you leave". Alfred felt a hand on his, he squeezed it.

Martha looked up then, and something moved behind her eyes. "We aren't going to be leaving. We will be staying. Or most of us anyway. Garth is heading back as you know", she indicated the ever-smiling musician, "but the rest of us", Martha said, hugging her other female friend, "will be staying. This is a resettlement mission. Your village is about to die. We are going to bring it back to life. Get these houses all sorted out. Make the gardens bigger. Bring a bit of life back". She laughed then. Alfred and Rebecca looked at each other then and smiled.

Martha went on. "We, Seacity, wants this village, funny as it may seem to you. This is one of the furthest settlements, so building it up again, would serve in many ways. As a marker of our land. But also, as a defence. Things have moved from the north before and may do again. We would like to know about this if they do." Alfred remembered then that tired traveller and his words but thought better of it for the moment. "I understand if you want to go. For you, this place is all you've ever known. And if you want to go, we will help you. You can go with Garth, and he can help you get set up in Seacity. Go to school maybe." She stopped then for a moment. Alfred noticed her eyes linger on Rebecca for a moment and seemed to start to say something but stopped herself. She shook her head a little before continuing. "But, if you want to stay and help and be part of this, we would love that. You two are this village really." She looked at them then, the fire flickering in her hazel eyes. And Rebecca looked at him too. Alfred couldn't think of anything to say. Everything had changed so quickly. Martha laughed suddenly. "I know this is a lot to take in. Don't worry, there is no rush. You have days, probably weeks, before Garth returns. We can talk a lot more about this.". They laughed again.

That night, for the first time in his life, Alfred got a little drunk. His memories were always broken ones, but he remembered people jumping over the fire, laughter and, at one point, Garth standing up, drunk, and to cheers and laughter, setting off for Seacity swaying on the saddle. At some point, he and Rebecca had weaved off into the night. Stars whirled around the night giddily. They had kissed then, increasingly hungrily, before Rebecca broke off and went laughing away.

3.

He was woken by screams. It was still dark, and it felt like only a short time had passed. Out of his window, he saw men galloping around the village, two of the huts already ablaze. A woman, Marth's friend, was being dragged out of the hut by her hair. Stunned, Alfred felt a tap on his shoulder. His father, with his fingers to his lips, beckoning him. They squatted down and ran as silently as possible to the other side of the room, where the window opened onto the black. A man, one of the raiders, burst in then, lit up from behind by the fires in the village. They were frozen like this for only an instant but, seeing them there, the man instantly ran at his father with a knife. Raising it above his head, he slashed downwards, striking his father on the shoulder. His father grabbed him, falling over on the floor. "Go" his father shouted at him as they fought there on the floor. "Go".

Alfred ran, jumping out of the window, crashing into Rebecca, who had just appeared. "Come on, let's go", she shouted at him, eyes big and wide and white. They ran then into the dark. The dark that had always seemed so vast and threatening, as if it was about to swallow them up, now seemed welcoming. They plunged into the deepest blackest part of the night, not daring to look behind them. They ran as hard and as far as they could, and slowly, slowly, the cries and shouts disappeared behind them.

They walked on in shock and fear for the rest of that night, hardly caring for the direction they took and sunrise found them cold and hungry. Walking to the top of a rise, they scanned the horizon. There was no sign of their village at first until Alfred spotted, a surprisingly long way away, a thin line of smoke rising straight up in the still air. Aside from that, the land was deserted.

"Do you think they're all dead?" he asked.

"Most of them. "Rebecca muttered. "Maybe they took some. I don't know."

"He was right then that man".

"Yes, we should have listened." There was nothing more to say.

Alfred looked then to the south. The thin line of green, that had always been visible on the clearest of days, now stood out much more prominently, an olive smudge of forest passing all across the horizon. The scale of it shocked Alfred. "It must be massive," he said.

"That's where they go, the travellers, right?" Rebecca asked.

"I think so, yes. They didn't say much but, yes, some mentioned the forest on the way to the Seacity. I think there are roads and paths they take."

"Well, come on then. It looks like we are going to Seacity after all," she said.

They walked for an hour or so until the day grew warmer then, exhausted, they found a flat piece of land behind some rocks. Lying down on the bare ground like animals, they were asleep in moments.

When Alfred awoke, Rebecca had her hand clamped on his mouth. She motioned him to be quiet. It was getting dark; they had slept most of the day. Then he heard them, voices, indistinct but close by. A woman's voice, pleading. Men laughing. There was a glow from a fire that seemed to come from the other side of the hill, and, as he gazed up, he could see embers float up and away and slowly die against the bluey black. He gazed into Rebecca's eyes. She motioned for him to follow her then, slowly and very quietly, she crept up the slope to the top. Joining her, Alfred peered over.

The slight rise sloped down to some flat ground where, not far away, probably only the length of their village, it rose again. On the far side, there was a large fire and, around it, in various places, were a group of men. Alfred looked at them. Some were bare chested; most wore a loose-fitting jacket. Their trousers were short and made of hide. Barefooted, their bodies marked with spirals and other swirling shapes. Not far away stood their horses.

Nearer to the fire were two women. One of them, the one Alfred had seen being attacked in the village, was lying down, not moving. The other though, sitting up, was, he realised, Martha. Alfred felt nauseous with horror. He watched transfixed - they seemed safe here for the moment. It was almost dark; they would be invisible against the glare of the fire, but for how long? As Alfred watched, one of the men approached Martha and kicked her in the face. She fell over backwards. He could hear the men's laughter. Rebecca suddenly hissed at him,

"Alfred, we need to go!"

"We can't leave her like this".

Rebecca looked at him. "Alfred", she simply said, eyes pleading. Alfred looked back, men were clustered around Martha now, on her. She was screaming.

They crept down the hillside and away till, at what they considered a safe distance, they broke into a run until they could no longer hear the screams.

"Bastards", Alfred gasped. "Bastards".

"Where are they going? What are they doing?" Rebecca asked.

"I don't know. Perhaps just rode out for a look around. For another village? They won't know the area, I don't think. It's a long time since they were down here".

"Do you think they'll go any further?"

"I don't know. Maybe. But they don't have enough to take Seacity, that's for sure. And their horses will be no good in the woods, I don't think. We'll head there".

The next few days were a blur. They mostly slept where they could in the day, walking at night when it was cooler, and they were more hidden. Not that they needed to hide. The landscape seemed empty. By the fourth day, they were in a bad way. Both were hobbling, though Rebecca, who had always struggled over longer distances, was worse. She didn't moan though, just pushed on, her face tight, lips clamped together. They were hungry but what was much worst was their thirst. Water was constantly on their mind. Whole hours of painful trudging went by where Alfred daydreamed of the poor little stream in their village, which now seemed a paradise in the memory.

His thoughts kept returning to what he had seen. He tried not to think of Martha. He decided he must turn away from that, or the darkness of it would enter him, rot inside, make him sick.

He thought of his father though. That last look he had given him. How he had fought the raider without thinking. How he had saved him. He thought of the years his father had hardly spoken a word to him, the physical beatings. Perhaps there was something here other than the cruelty and negligence Alfred had long decided on, a knowledge that had festered within him. He tried to go as far back as he could, to when his mother was alive. He had a memory of them in the garden. Laughter. There was a mystery and a sadness here that Alfred knew he would never fathom.

The landscape had changed. It was flatter now, with many more grasses and bushes and trees growing. They constantly sucked and chewed on the leaves of these for moisture, but it was more torture than sustenance. They couldn't see far ahead now; Alfred hoped the forest proper was only another night or so walking ahead.

One night, a little way ahead of Rebecca, Alfred heard the unmistakable trickle of water. "Rebecca", he croaked, "water". They painfully followed the sound, ears straining in the dark till Alfred almost stumbled into it. They both immediately fell to their knees in it, drinking till their belly's felt like bursting. They were both sick, but then, afterwards, pale and shaking, they just lay down and drank again. Finally getting their fill, they hobbled along downstream till the sun came up and, when it finally did, warming and drying their wet bodies and clothes, they felt better than they could have imagined a few hours ago.

Refreshed by the water, they didn't immediately plunge into unconsciousness like on previous nights, but lay on the gravel feeling the luxurious pleasure of the warm sun soaking into them. Alfred felt the play of Rebecca's hand on his and his mind swam back to that kiss. It seemed a lifetime ago, although only a few days had passed. He turned over to her. Her face was close, looking straight at him. Alfred reached out for her hair, pulling her closer, mouths meeting hungrily.

They slept deeply that day, bodies entwined in the sun till they had the sense to lay their clothes over themselves to stop their skin from burning. They woke up in the evening and made a fire. There was plenty of dry bush around to use and, metal and flints were plentiful enough, as usual, to cause a spark. The fire roared up all night and, as crabs scuttled out of the cold, dank mud for their nightly hunting, they caught and roasted them over the fire.

On the next day, they weren't quick to start. They stripped and washed in the lovely clear water; the river ran much faster and fresher than the lazy muddy one they knew from home. Alfred felt born anew, walking naked out of the stream into the sun.

The river ran in their direction of travel, southwards towards the forest and, without ever speaking of their decision, they followed it, never veering far from the security of its shores. They walked slowly and not very far that day, stopping to rest and swim in the midday heat. The afternoon found them walking through a hot, flat land made more pleasant by the increasing numbers of bushes that started to crowd the riverside casting their shade onto them.

It was Rebecca that noticed it first. 'Urgh', she wrinkled her face. A stench of death filled the air. It grew stronger, causing them to cover their faces with their arms and then Rebecca stopped a few yards from where flies buzzed frantically over some black rags. Toeing it cautiously, Alfred uncovered bones with rags of flesh attached. Beetles toiled over the carcass industriously. Around the middle was a belt clasped with a silver buckle.

"Has he been here long?" Rebecca said eventually.

"He must have. It's that traveller I told you about" Alfred toed delicately, the silver buckle. "It's been months and months since he left. I'm surprised there is anything still left of him".

"Perhaps he didn't travel directly here. They wander about doing what they do, don't they?"

"I'm not sure with this one. He wanted to get to Seacity".

Near the man was his bag of 'findings', as the travellers called it. Alfred looked inside. Although he had been able to snatch quick looks many times in his role at the inn, he had never been given free rein to poke around and have a good look. This traveller's haul was mostly metal. He had seen some with solely plastic. Perhaps they specialised in what they collected, he thought? This traveller's haul was the best he'd ever seen, or at least the most beautiful, as he still didn't know really what was of any actual worth or use. Bars of burnished bronze hardly pitted at all. A square plate of something that showed green in the sun. But what took his eye most was the gold. Some chunks of it like his fist. He took one and held it. He loved the weight of it, how it glowed in the sun. It felt warm in his hand.

"Get some, Rebecca. It might come in useful." She got a piece too, smaller, rounder, almost like a coin.

"How did he die, do you think?" he asked.

Who knows?" she said. "Perhaps he sickened of something. Perhaps something bit him". They had both disturbed several snakes this morning. One had refused to move out of their way as they usually did but loitered, languishing in the sun. Orange stripes licked around the thick coils of its burnished body that writhed slowly as they watched. They had given it a wide berth.

They travelled then, a few hours more, stopping in time to make a large fire. Again they fed well, then feasted luxuriously on the curves and swells of each other before sleep took them.

They awoke to bird song. They had seen the odd bird around their village, but not many. They mainly had been desultory, small brown things that pecked at the ground without much interest before flying off. Here though, the blue sky seemed filled with the noise of them, all different sounds. Fluting noises, sharp chip chips. Harsh caws. They lay there and looked up in wonder for a long time before the noise started to lessen. Birds flashed by in a blaze of blue along the river. A big, bold one sat nearby on a branch and sang its heart out, chest puffed out in proud gold and chestnut.

They had almost thought themselves in the forest, so bushy and overgrown to their eyes had the land become. But an hour or so later, when they turned a corner, they had realised their mistake. There it stood, a thick, tall green wall. They stopped in awe. They approached slowly, almost fearful. The brown trunks of the trees gradually grew more real and massive than they ever could have imagined.

They hesitated there, at the edge of the forest. Through the branches, shafts of light pierced the gloom, filled with the innumerable flitting of thousands of insects. They looked at each other, took each other's hand and walked in, following the river as it slipped quietly into the wood.

The change was immediate. Cooler. Darker. They walked on, hardly daring to make a noise. Trees soared above them where, high above, Alfred could make out large colourful birds flying. There was rustling and the odd louder crash in the growth around them that startled them the first few times it happened but, turning, they saw it was just small birds bustling through the undergrowth. They followed the river, that slipped clean and straight, deeper and deeper into the green.

Whereas before they knew they had been travelling south, they now quickly became disorientated. It was just possible to make out where the sun was, high above the countless millions of leaves and branches. However, they were still scared to leave the safety of the river, after their previous experience, and clung to its side, even as it meandered daily more westwards. The forest lay all about, massive and uncaring. As they travelled deeper, they started to see more animals, eyes and bodies attuning to this new environment. Animals they had no name for. Animals that jumped from branch to branch. Animals that peered out at them, nose and ears twitching, poised on four delicate legs, wide-eyed, till, curiosity satisfied, they padded off into the shadows.

Alfred and Rebecca thought there must be larger animals here. Something lurked deep inside both of them, some trace memory of beasts that could chase them, tear at them, eat them, but they saw no sign. At night though, they listened to the constant creaks and rustles around them, their imaginations bringing forth all manner of creatures with claws and teeth and poison that they thought watched them even now, as they lay.

Thinking this, they gradually moved closer and closer to the small fire they kept burning all night.

Hunger quickly became an issue again. The easy prey of crabs they had depended on had vanished with the new habitat. They had managed to catch some fish from time to time, blocking the river with rocks to trap them, and it was this that had sustained them for, though they saw life everywhere, it was forever out of reach.

They had tried to run down the animals they had seen, but that had been an embarrassing affair. The larger beasts hardly bothered to break into a trot. The smaller ones vanished into the growth with a crash, or simply skittered up the nearest tree then gazing, tauntingly, down at them from the nearest branch.

They thought of, and planned, numerous traps as they walked, but neither had the knowledge or skill or, they thought, the time to put these into use. Their attempts around the fire in the evening to fashion something were usually laughable, and, in the morning, they were always empty.

So, they gradually grew hungrier and hungrier, but still they pressed on, ever deeper into the forest. It was all they felt they could do.

Four days had passed in the forest when Rebecca, who was walking slightly ahead of Alfred, suddenly stopped. 'Look at that, she said, pointing. Alfred looked. The river curved to the right here. Slightly in front of them, a small path, grass bent and flattened, ran upwards from the river to their left.

"It could be animals?" Alfred suggested. Rebecca didn't reply. 'Let's have a little look", he said, "Quiet'. They took the path and crept in single file. Rebecca hadn't gone too far when she stopped and crouched down behind a trunk. Alfred joined her.

Ahead, in a clearing, was a house. It was quite large and rambling and seemed made in different sections. Smoke curled out of a chimney. There was a large garden and a fence and, inside it were some large pinkish animals snouting away in the earth. "What are those?" Alfred asked. Rebecca shook her head.

A mule stood tethered to a pole. "Isn't that Jasper?" Rebecca asked. She was right, it was, Alfred was sure of that. Alfred hadn't seen too many mules, but that this was identical to Jasper, was Jasper, he was convinced: a shaggy mottled brown, a shock of white on its fetlocks.

Suddenly, Rebecca's hand clutched his arm. The door opened on the house and out walked the occupant. He was old. Older than anyone, he thought, that he had ever seen, but, for all that, stronger and more able. Although small, he walked without impairment over to the garden and fussed over the animals for a while. He was clad in a variety of colourful rags and, even though they were some distance away, they could hear him mumbling and singing little snatches of song. They stayed there and observed for a good while. There was no other occupant, it seemed, just this little, old man.

"We should go see him," Alfred said.

"What?" Rebecca replied.

"We should go see him. He might be able to help us".

"Well, he might", Rebecca concurred, "but he also might not. He might be dangerous. Why does he have Garth's mule? And where is Garth?" She was right; where was Garth? Alfred thought back fondly of Garth. The thought though, that that tall, powerful man would have been in any threat from this creeping old fool seemed laughable.

"That old man couldn't have done anything to Garth. Maybe Garth bartered the horse. And anyway, I don't think we have much choice. We don't have any food. We don't know where we are going."

Rebecca thought on this. It was hard to argue with. "Well, one of us should stay here," she said, reluctantly, after a few moments consideration. "Watch. Be ready to help."

"Ok. Well, I'll go. I'll be careful. I won't be long. You stay here".

"Here, take this," she said and slipped a piece of metal she had secreted from somewhere into his hand. It sat cupped there quite nicely, one end smooth and rounded against the palm, the other sharp and jagged. "I'll wait here. Don't be long".

Alfred stood up and walked out into the opening. He was prepared to approach the old man unnoticed for a while and then hail him, but he was surprised that, even at a distance, as a branch cracked under his foot, the man immediately straightened up and looked at him.

"Hello," Alfred said foolishly, waving an arm. "Hello." The old man still said nothing, just looked.

"Who are you?" he simply said, and the forest seemed to suddenly silence.

"I'm a survivor of the raids", Alfred rattled out the story he had agreed upon with Rebecca. "I'm lost. I need some help". The old man approached a little.

"Yes, the raids. I've heard about them. There will be more. You come from the north?" Alfred nodded.
The man grunted and shook his head. "Well, you did well to survive. Not many do." He suddenly stopped then and barked, "You're alone?", keen eyes scanning the forest.

Alfred prayed Rebecca was well hidden. 'Oh yes, all alone. Just me". The old man searched the forest for a moment then, seeming satisfied at his response, he looked back at Alfred. His demeanour suddenly changed back to that of the harmless, old man Alfred had observed before.

"Well then, come 'ere, come inside, I dare say you'll be wanting a bite", he opened the door to the shack. Alfred paused. "Come in, come in, I won't bite". The old man stood at the side of the door, grinning. He still seemed to have a full set of teeth Alfred noticed, which none of the old people ever did in his village, gumming at whatever vegetables or meat they could lay their hands on.

Alfred walked into the house, ducking under a bundle of some herbs tied at the top of the door. It was dark, only a little light able to make its way inside. In the middle of the large room was a fire which smouldered dull and red. The room was crammed with objects. Sacks of metal and plastic. A bird in a cage hung from the ceiling looked at Alfred with its large, orange eye.

The man walked into the room, chuckling to himself, went to a table and lit a candle. He brushed off some dust and bits of wood off one of the chairs, "come sit, sit ", he urged. "Hungry, I expect?" That Alfred could not deny. The man went to a large pot hung over the fire, put a large ladleful of the contents into a bowl, then placed it before Alfred. It was brown and pungent. Steam rolled off it. "Go on, go on", the man urged.

Alfred did. It tasted delicious after days of not much but crab and fish. The man seemed delighted by this, giggling to himself. "Go on lad, fill yourself up, there's more where that came from." A drink was placed before him in a mug, herbs of some sort inside. "Do you good that will. Make you strong. Drink." Alfred did so. The man chattered on, more to himself at times it seemed than anything that needed a response from Alfred.

"So you're from the north, are you?" he eventually asked him. "You look healthy for one of them. What is it that's wrong with you, I wonder?" The man peered at him intently. Despite his age, his blue eyes seemed clear and focused. "Hmm. Can't see anything. Must be something though. Now then, what will it be that you are wanting from me. Help, I expect in some way".

"Well, yes. If you can. I'd like to get to Seacity. I'm lost". The man cackled at this.

"Seacity, he says, Seacity! A mutie wants to go to Seacity. Funny my boy, that". The boy wondered at the old man, for now his features seemed to be sharper, skin tauter, younger somehow. "Seacity is a long way away, boy. And it's a dangerous place. No, you'd be better staying here with old John, I think. Plenty of food to eat here. Plenty of things to do.". The man must have started to sense Alf shift away as he leaned closer, more intently. "Oh yes, and safe too, my boy. No raiders won't come down here. They never have, never will. No good for men on horses, you see. No one bothers with us here. There's just the forest. And the forest is good for those who knows it". Alfred had long since finished the drink and the stew. He thought of Rebecca outside. He longed now to be gone from here. Alfred felt a panic start to well up inside him and desperately tried to control it.

"Well, that's good and kind of you John, but, yes, Seacity is where I want to go. I'll be okay there, I'm sure. I have a name. A traveller who passed through".

"A name he says," John scoffed, standing up. He was becoming more animated all the time. "Well, I'm sure he may have passed through but whether he ever got to Seacity at all is a different matter. He may well be dead boy, did you ever think of that?". Alfred looked at the floor. He wanted to be gone now. He stood up, a table between him and John.

"Well, I'll thank you for your drink and your food. Most kind of you. But I will be going now. I would be grateful if you could send me in the right direction". John stood staring at him from the other side of the table. Alfred was loath to take his eyes from him.

"You're going the right way," he said softly. "Or the easiest at least. Keep following the river, which I'm assuming you have followed here, and it will take you to a large track in a day or two. Turn south on that, and that's that."

"Well, thank you." Alfred turned to go. But he was held by something, and he couldn't leave without asking. "The horse out there. I recognise it. I knew the man who owned it. Did he lend it you?". There was a moment then when John's eyes changed, narrowed, lidded with suspicion. Then, with a freakish speed, the old man was on him. His hands gripped his arms with a strength that scared Alfred. There was no way he could even think of resisting this. He was helpless.

"That man", John's face was contorted by anger, spitting as he spoke, "is dead. I killed him. And you've eaten him", a hideous smile breaking out on his face. Alfred felt the horror loom up on him and swallow him. And suddenly, all seemed lost and finished and gone. John gripped him with both hands, a terrible smile on his face. And then a scuffle and a bang, and John was on the floor, eyes dazed, blood starting to trickle out of one ear. And Rebecca was standing there, breathing heavily, her knuckles clenched white on the pan she was holding.

They stood there in shock a moment. John stared up at them, his neck held tight and straining up from the floor, eyes going from one to the other. He started to make a noise then, as if trying to speak, louder and louder.

"What's up with him?" Alf said.

"I don't know. We need to go."

"We should help him."

"No. Come on, let's go. He's dangerous. And he's a bad man. Let's just go." Alfred gave in then to the fear, and they ran then out of the house towards the path. "Wait". He said. And turning to Jasper, he untied him and took him by the rope down the path towards the river. Reaching it, they turned and listened. Silence. Bird song. They carried on up the river, Rebecca leading Jasper. They walked quickly for hours, and it was long after the house had disappeared from view that they dared to speak.

Alfred told Rebecca what the man had said regarding the direction of Seacity. Alfred argued that that at least was true, for what would be the advantage to the old man of any lie in it?

"Malice", Rebecca merely replied. But still, they carried on as before as leaving the river seemed folly.

They walked for two days. Although there was the odd section where a fallen branch or bog made for a slight detour with Jasper, on the whole, the going was easy. Rebecca rode on his back for a few hours each day, and they fussed over the horse, stopping at what looked to them would be the choicest, lushest bits of vegetation for a horse. They talked little of what lay behind them but often, with increasing excitement, of Seacity.

The knowledge and existence of Seacity had been, perhaps, the one thing of the outside world that their city had managed to retain. What little scraps of information that had been passed on to the children, they had long since furnished with their imagination. That it still thrived as a seat of learning and commerce was apparent from what Martha and the others had said. Even, it seemed possible, starting to reach out again. They talked of this, talked of paved streets, and shops, and schools, and towers, and high walls and soldiers. Alfred's thoughts though, often turned to what was behind the wall on that far side. And even though he had never seen a picture of the sea, his mind furnished from somewhere inside him a vision of an infinite blue of crashing waves, and birds that swooped over them, and wondrous things that swam within its deeps.

On the third day, not long after setting off, Alfred noticed a thinning in the trees ahead. Then suddenly, with no warning, the path ahead of them curved round to the right and, incredibly, they were out, the trees opening above them, onto a wider, sandy track. The river they had been following all this time ran across this track, where it dipped slightly, across a broader, shallow passage of stones, then slipped quietly and darkly into the forest on the other side where it quickly disappeared.

It was good to see the sky again. The track cut straight across, north to south, before disappearing into the thick, green gloom in both directions. Alfred remembered the old man's instructions. Turn right. Head south. And that did feel the right way to go.

"Look here," Rebecca said. Alfred looked closer. Footprints could be seen. Hoof marks. They didn't seem too old. They looked at each other with a smile, and their hunger and tiredness seemed to fade away. After their days in the waste and forest, it all seemed so easy now.

They set off, Rebecca riding on Jasper. The wide sandy floor seemed perfect for horses. With such easy going, a blue sky overhead, the path stretching before them, they chatted easily and lightly. For both, it seemed that they had completed the hard part of the journey.

It wasn't long until they saw a tumbledown wooden structure ahead of them. "Look," Rebecca said, pointing, but Alfred had already seen it. It was large and seemed larger still as they approached, larger than any building they had ever seen. They stopped a little way from it. There were obvious signs of life, distant noises, the odd voice. Smoke from the chimney. A log pile on the side of the building.

"It should be ok," Rebecca said. "This is on the main road. People must pass regularly. It probably serves travellers. Like your house did."

"Yes", Alfred replied hesitantly. That made sense, of course. They went on. Arriving at the building they found the door open, and, inside, they could see a few tables set out, with what seemed a serving area towards the rear. With her back towards them, a woman dressed in red and white seemed to be bustling over something. She was singing. As they watched, Rebecca nudged him. From where they had walked, a cart now trundled into view being hauled by a horse.

They walked in, tying up Jasper on the post outside. The woman, hearing their approach, stood up and turned. "Hello," she said, taking them in in a glance. Her face was lined and thin, yellowish hair hanging down. There were stains on her clothes. Whatever she thought, she didn't say. "Take a seat, and I'll be over."

They sat down. This was an entirely novel experience for both of them. A large bearded man came out from a door to the rear, a large knife in his belt. He went over to the woman, saying something. In the corner of the room was a flight of stairs and, above, they could hear footsteps clattering around, children's voices.

The woman came over. "We have stew on today. Beer. Kava. Some bread and cheese." She looked at them, taking them in. "Do you have any coin on you?".

"No, we don't", Alfred went on. He saw the woman's face sour then, saw that she was about to say something. Alfred suddenly thought of the gold he had but Rebecca beat him to it, producing the smaller gold piece that she had taken. Alfred watched the woman and saw, for a moment, the shock this produced, the sudden gleam in her eyes. She controlled herself quickly though and, carefully, went on in as neutral a voice as she could.

"Yes, that will do", smiling then for the first time. She reached out and took the coin, still looking at them. "You two just sit here". They watched as she bustled off. For a moment, as the door swung open to the rear, Alfred saw her approach the man hurriedly and her whisper something to him, and him quickly turning around, dark eyes meeting Alfred's for a moment before the door swing closed.

"That was too much", Alfred hissed.

"Well, at least we know now. And we have yours, of course. And it will give us food and drink, and that is what we need more than any gold." Alfred felt Rebecca's hand take his. They heard the cart arrive outside, the heavy clop of the horse, saw it thrash its head around in the leather leads that attached it. Both stared at the animal – they had never seen a large horse like this before, only stunted mules. A whole family came in. Two boys, both with yellow hair, walked in first. They seemed familiar with the place and how it worked and walked easily over to a table, talking and laughing. The man and woman came next, both thin but dressed in clean, simple clothes. Alfred noticed both their eyes take them in as they sat down.

The large bearded man came out then with the food. He stood by their table and handed over the steaming plates and two large glasses of beer. The tense quiet surrounding the man made Alfred uncomfortable, and it made him think of his father. He saw then, for the first time since it happened, his father locked in battle with the raider, the raider's hand coming down. Blood. He grimaced and, with an effort, turned away from it.

Both were silent then for a good while, bodies and minds turned to the steaming nutritious mush and beer before them. Alfred felt he could feel the strength and life of it go straight into his body. The beer, stronger and better than they were used to, went quickly to their heads. After finishing the one, Rebecca, taking a chance, asked for another one. There was no complaint, no request for payment. Both realised that they must have handed over a significant sum. Alfred thought then and, signalling the man, he said, with a feigned confidence that the beer was assisting with, "two more plates of this please". Again, the man did a faint brusque nod and, taking their empty plates, returned to the kitchen. They were elated at this sudden feast.

"Hungry, eh?" a man's voice broke in. Alfred looked over to the nearby table. The man's face was not an unkindly one, a faint smile in a lined face. The same yellow hair as his sons. "Yes. We were both ready for this," Alfred replied. Rebecca, he noticed, had raised her glass to the man, which he copied in an attempt at comfortable bonhomie. The man smiled again and raised his.

"You're heading to Seacity, I imagine?".

"We are", Alfred replied. There seemed little point in evasion. The man laughed, "I would have been more curious if you weren't. That's where everyone goes. That's where the road goes. That's where we're going." He again looked them over, seeming to take them in. "A long way on foot still. You've only got one horse?".

"We'll manage," Alfred said.

"Oh, I've no doubt of that", he returned. And smiling, he returned then to his family and their meal.

Alfred and Rebecca finished off their meal and their drink. It felt good to be warm and safe and full. The road stretched ahead of them to Seacity, and all they needed to do was stay on it. They stood to leave just as the other family finished. The father, as they readied to go, approached them then. "Listen," he said, "We are both going the same way. We have a large wagon. And you have a horse and two people. It would seem sensible to me, to share." He stopped. Alfred and Rebecca said nothing. He laughed a little then. "We can attach your horse to the wagon. That will make the going easier and also give us both insurance if anything goes wrong with either horse. And you get a free ride". He smiled. "Seems like a good deal to me".

Perhaps at another time, even an hour before, their response would have been different, but, with the sun shining, and a belly full of food and drink, there seemed little to fear. "Yes," they both said at the same time. Rebecca went on. "That does sound a good plan. Yes, let's do it".

And it was a good plan. They took their seats in the open wagon with the two boys, the man and the woman upfront. The family were curious about them, and, slowly, they teased most of their story out of them, leaving out only the details of the violence of the raid. And the old man in the forest. Both were reluctant to tell how they had left him there on the floor.

The husband and wife didn't seem surprised. "Everyone is talking of this. The raids. We are lucky. Our village is not so north as yours. The first we heard of this was from the travellers who passed through before. We are used to tall tales from them, but they all spoke of this. And all of them were heading south, none heading north. Well, such tales are strange to us, from the long ago. But there seemed to us to be only one decision."

"You've left?".

"Yes." The man went on. "This is everything", he motioned to the wagon and the horse. "Not much for a lifetime of hard work", a wry smile. "Oh, we still have our house back there, but I imagine someone will already be in that. Still, I think we will have the better of the deal. In the stories I remember, the raiders didn't just appear once then vanish. They raided all of the lands north of the woods for years and years. They'll be back, I think, and soon. We hope to be in Seacity by then."

The days passed pleasantly. There was the odd shower during which they took shelter under the overhanging boughs of the green forest that crowded on either side, but mostly the sun shone. The family became more friendly and shared their food with them. They passed the odd traveller on foot heading south, a few with horses heading north.

The third day started like the others. They were in high spirits. The sun was shining high ahead. The family hadn't travelled this road before but, their village being closer, were more familiar with it from talk of more numerous travellers and traders. Two more days, the man and woman thought, and they would be clear of the forest. And then only another day or two until finally, incredibly, they would be at Seacity!

They were talking excitedly of their plans for their arrival when, rounding a slight, long curving bend, the wagon slowed to a halt and stopped. "What is it," Rebecca asked, then fell silent. They looked over to where the man and woman, Guthrir and Eline, were looking.

Not far away, perhaps as far as Alfred could throw a stone, there was a carcass of some sort on the path. Something big. Fur. Skin. Bones. A massive animal was squatted on it, its head inside of what remained. They could see the strength of it from where they were, each twist and bite of it, moving the corpse violently. The animal looked up and gazed at them for a moment, blood covered its muzzle. Everyone held their breath. It returned to the meal in front of it, uninterested. "Bear", one of the boys hissed beside them. The existence of such massive beasts caused Alfred's head to spin. He was dimly aware of the existence of large animals in forests but, having seen no trace of any through all the time they had been there, had started to think of the forest as a largely harmless place. Alfred felt cold, realising that they must have been close to some of these animals all the time they had travelled alone. Perhaps they had simply just got lucky. There didn't seem any particular danger now though. The bear seemed content to feast on what was in front of him. Having such a full belly, Alfred doubted whether it would cause any threat to them as long as they gave it a wide berth. But how were they to get around it? There wasn't space to go past anywhere on the side?

After some debate, the decision was reached to stay put. It seemed too troublesome to even think of getting the waggon through the forest. "We'll stay here", Guthrir had said. "When it's eaten, it'll move off. And we're in no rush". There was indeed no rush. They had food and water. The bear seemed little threat, though they retreated a bit further down the road just in case and turned the cart around in case they had to set off at a trot. Guthrir and Eline were to keep a close eye on it, and they would simply move on when it eventually moved off into the woods.

They talked of animals while they waited. The family were astonished, then amused, to learn of Alfred and Rebecca's ignorance of such things. "You mean you haven't heard of a bear," Eline asked incredulously, the two young boys, delighting in their ignorance, teasing them. Laughing, the children went through other animals of the forest that these strange travellers might also be ignorant of. Alfred struggled to visualise a wolf, unable to picture a massive, snarling version of Harald.

They were still laughing when Alfred felt Guthrir move on his seat, "oh oh, what's this?". Alfred turned to look back down the road. Out of the mass of fur that they had assumed was just one animal, a little, lighter coloured clot had disentangled itself and was busy skipping and tumbling around, seemingly trying to capture insects. Another one appeared, and they both tumbled around. There were two cubs! They must have been dozing on the other side of what they now assumed to be Mum. Alfred smiled. It was lovely to watch them playing. Then, as they watched, one of the bear cubs suddenly froze, looking in their direction. Then the other cub, turning to look where his sibling was, froze also, sniffing the air.

They all laughed. It was comical to watch two little cubs be on such severe alert at their presence while mum was clearly disinterested. Suddenly, one of the cubs sprang towards them and started to bound in their direction. They laughed, but as the animal got closer, the horses, which had remained surprisingly calm throughout, began to jerk in their traces. The family's horse, Sally, as the cub got closer, started to jump up on its forelegs and pound its feet down, shaking the wagon from side to side.

The laughing stopped. The woman struggled with the reins trying to calm the horses down, get them to move, but the bear cub was on them now, nipping at the horses' feet, sending the wagon from side to side. Suddenly, Alfred heard a roar from behind, and, turning, the mother bear, aware now of what she saw as a threat, was charging incredibly swiftly towards them. At that moment, the horses bolted, the sudden speed and angle of their movement tipping over the cart.

Alfred was on the floor in a tumble of noise and confusion. The bear had passed him and was biting at Jasper's flank, the horse screaming and falling over. As he watched, the man, who was closer to the bear, started to crawl over towards them. The bear, noticing this, picked up the man by his neck and ran a few paces away, thrashing him from side to side. The man had his arms around the bear's massive head and was screaming terribly. Alfred found himself holding Eline with one hand, Rebecca on the other, running away up the road, the boys already ahead of them running wildly. They turned back for a moment. Behind them, he saw the man's body on the road, still. The bear was now busy with the horses, which still screamed, trapped in the traces of the wagon.

They all ran till they no longer could. Stopping exhausted, Alfred was sick, heaving up his guts till he wondered at what he could possibly be bringing up. Eline was pale, and shivered in a blanket taken from the wagon, the boys sobbing, pulling at her. Rebecca was holding them, trying to soothe them. They walked then. They had no food or water, no bedding or shelter. The boys' sobs gave way in time to a strange silence, echoing their mother, who seemed struck dumb. But they walked without complaint, huddling by the side of the road when darkness took them, staying close to the fire which Alfred kept well stoked all night. The next day they met some travellers going north and told them of the bear. The travellers spared them some biscuits in return. Told them they weren't far now from the edge of the forest and the first villages.

The end of the forest came the next day. It came quite suddenly, the track opening up in front of them, the forest pulling back. A large village lay in front of them that the road disappeared in to. For one moment, Rebecca had thought it Seacity, but Elina, breaking her silence for the first time since the incident, had just looked at them then and shook her head. "That's not Seacity", she had simply said.

They walked through the village, the villagers taking little notice of them. From there on, it was a country of open fields and little woods and villages every few miles. In the next village, some of the children had followed them out and, half-heartedly, thrown some stones at Rebecca. "Mutie", they had shouted. Alfred was furious and threw the stones back violently, till Rebecca had stopped him with a hand on his arm. " 'Mutie'", he had said, "What do they mean by that?!" Elina just looked up at him, and then Rebecca, with her dark limpid eyes, then looked away.

That night they slept in a barn that no one seemed to be using. They awoke to a clear day, and there, in front of them, no more than a few miles away, were visible the turrets and towers of Seacity against the rosy dawn. It was the most beautiful thing Alfred had ever seen.

They walked towards it all morning, the stream of traffic slowly growing bigger, carts of produce heading towards the city, empty ones returning. It seemed an almost continuous settlement now, of houses fringing the road. The towers rose steadily in front of them, until, finally, there it stood across a clearing, grey walls stretching off to either side.

Alfred looked at them. They were as tall as the trees that had hemmed them in for so long. Ahead stretched the path to the gate where some men in uniform stood apparently on guard. As he watched, he saw them speak to a woman and then let her proceed in through the massive gates that were half-open. The houses that followed the path for so long stopped here. It seemed Seacity desired a large, open stretch around its border wall.

Alfred's eyes travelled up the wall to the towers that clustered and soared behind it. Large birds with swept up wings circled around them. In the background, a hum of noise could now be heard, the hum of the city. To his right, beyond the sweep of the wall, the land levelled off flat and bare. A line of blue. The sea!

They looked at each other, smiling. Elina still had her head down; she was very pale. The boys clutched on to her on either side. Alfred felt a pang of pity. She should be coping better with her grief, he thought. Perhaps there would be doctors who could take care of her in the city?

They set off across the gap. The road was the busiest they had seen it. There was traffic behind them, and, ahead, it looked like a bustle of traffic was just passing through. By chance however, it seemed like they had timed their arrival for a momentary quiet, and they felt conspicuous and increasingly nervous as they walked across the divide. The guards didn't seem particularly troubled by their approach. Three of them were talking and laughing, one of them sat on a seat. They didn't appear in a state of high alert. As they got slowly closer though, the two nearest them started to pay more attention, looking them over as they arrived.

came to a stop as they reached them. It seemed the thing to do, though they weren't exactly blocking their way. Alfred could see the hustle and bustle of the city just a few paces ahead. People walking this way and that. A stall selling fruit.

"Hello," Alfred said and then felt foolish.

"Hello," the guard replied. "You've come far, it looks like".

"Yes. From the north," Alfred replied. It didn't seem like the time to lie. On that word' north', the guard looked up at him. He noticed that the other guard close by, who hadn't seem particularly interested, suddenly stood more upright and walked in front of them, blocking his view of the city.

"The North". The guard repeated. "All of you?". They nodded. "What about you?" he said to the woman. Elina, who had hardly said a word the last few days, replied, "Grunweld". The guard seemed satisfied with that and beckoned her through. She walked into the city then, her two sons clutching on, and disappeared into the throng. Alfred never saw them again
"You two also?" They shook their head. Alfred often wondered what would have happened if they had simply just nodded.

"No. Further north."

The man looked up again at them and, this time, held their gaze a little longer. The other guards, Alfred noticed, had now approached and looked silently on.

"What's the name of your town" the one who had stood quietly during this asked. They looked at each other. It seemed suddenly very odd that they had never thought of that. It had always just been their home. "Er, I don't know," Alfred replied. "It wasn't a town really. Just a few houses".

The guards mumbled something between themselves. "How long have you been travelling for," the first man asked.

"Two weeks, I suppose". Alfred replied. The man's eyes narrowed. It wasn't a cruel face. The green eyes looked at him, open and unguarded.

"These are from the far North", one of the other guards said, approaching them. Alfred noticed that two guards now stood to one side and were dealing, with much less fuss, the other travellers who approached and then went through the gates. They were, it seemed, something of a special case. The guard went on. "The mutie zone". 'Mutie', that word again. "You heard anything about raiders?" the guard asked quietly.

"Yes, we were attacked", Rebecca who had stood quietly to this point, said.

All the guards looked at them then. "So it is true," one said in a quiet voice.

"So you have escaped to Seacity for a new life?" The first guard went on.

"Yes." That was, of course, what they were doing. The other one approached him closer now. He had been pacing around behind them. "She won't be able to come in, Gerald," he said. "She's a mutie". Rebecca and Alfred looked at each other in alarm. "Nor him, for now at least. He looks ok. But there are the rules."

They looked to the guard.

"You don't know any of this, do you?"

They didn't say anything. Alfred shook his head.

"It's an old law. But it's one we still have. It's hardly ever used as we hardly see anyone like you anymore." The guard looked up at the sky for a moment then continued, not unkindly. "Where you live is contaminated. Or it has been. It's been a long time." He looked away. "Someone needs to explain all this properly to you. I'm rushing. But, yes, he's right that we are not allowed to let anyone in from where you live who shows signs of poisoning." He motioned to Rebecca.

Alfred felt light-headed and far away. He then looked at Rebecca though and, for the first time, he saw her as he suddenly realised everyone else did. Her right side of her body was withered. Her arm, whilst able still, was noticeably smaller than her left. Her leg was worse affected though. She had always limped. He noticed her hip bulged out, maybe in trying to compensate for her weakened leg. A rush of memories then of childhood, her limping behind, her dropping back as they chased Harald, the children throwing stones at them. And what was it Martha had said? Rebecca, he noticed, was looking at the floor. Alfred stumbled on. "But Harald had said…." for some reason then, he thought of Harald from all that time ago. And, as Alfred thought back to Harald and what he had said, he retrieved from his pocket the token that had been there for so long, deep in a tight inner fold of the cloth, that his fingers went so automatically to it every day that he had almost forgotten to think of it as a thing, something separate to him. He thought then and pulled it out. Held it out on his palm. "Here," he said simply, "Harald said he might be known by this."

When he thought back on this in later years, that moment always seemed strangely frozen. A boy with his hand out. Upon which lay a small dull red token, and there, uppermost, the simple engraved image of a man hauling a sack. The guards clustered around. "It's a mark," said one of them in a low voice.

"Where did you get this boy?" asked the guard who had been speaking to him.

"Harald he was called", Alfred explained. "He said this was his mark, and I should show it and ask for him." The guard looked up at him and smiled wryly.

"Well, he told you that right. Wait here".

Alfred and Rebecca were ushered to the side, sitting in the shade while the guards carried on their work. But they didn't have to wait long. Long before an hour was out, a man appeared out of the gates with a guard leading them on. Alfred could hear the guard speaking to him as they approached, "here they are, master".

Alfred recognised him but only just. Gone was the weather-beaten figure dressed in dusty robes from those years before; here was a man in a resplendent olive green garb, clasped with a black belt of good leather and metal. But his eyes were still the same as he remembered, kindly and blue in a face that was still tanned and lined.

"Alfred", he simply said. A note of wonder in his voice. "You came?".

Alfred looked up. Harald. His throat tightened. "Yes" was all he could say.

Harald smiled then, shaking his head, his eyes wide with wonder. "And you still had the mark after all this time". He laughed. "I remember laughing at my foolishness as I walked away. I thought I must have been touched by the sun to trust a young boy with a mark, still.....here you are." He turned then to Rebecca.

"The guards have spoken to you, they tell me" she nodded. Harald sighed. "In truth, it is a cruelty that I don't care for, but don't worry. You won't be able to come inside the city. At least not yet. It's an old and tired law. Not always observed now in truth but, for now," he lowered his voice a little, the guards didn't seem to be listening, but they weren't far away, " we must play the game". He smiled at them "Alfred, you can come with me", he said.

"I won't leave Rebecca", Alfred broke in, the horrible truth starting to dawn on him. Harald went to say something, but Rebecca then spoke up, placing her hand on his arm.

"Alfred, just go," she said, smiling. "It's Seacity. It's meant for you." He looked at her, and he could feel the tears starting.

"But you...."

Harald then intervened. "I know a place. A farm. A nice place with a nice family not far from here. I've used it before. Their last help has recently gone and they would be happy to have a girl such as you, I'm sure." Alfred went to say something again, but Harald went on. "This won't be forever," he said. "Rebecca is right, Alfred. To come so far and not come in. No – that can't be. And this situation with Rebecca – it won't be forever you can trust me on that. And you'll be able to see her. After a few days, once we have you settled in so you can come and go as you please, you can visit each other as much as you like. It wouldn't be more than half a days journey."

The discussion went on a little more, but that really was that. In later years Alfred wondered over his actions. He wondered how he had allowed a guard to lead Rebecca off while he walked the other way with Harald (albeit after tears and promises made). Why, indeed, he let them be separated without too much of an argument. Why hadn't he just gone to live with Rebecca till it had all been sorted out? He wondered too over Harald's advice. Perhaps he had just made a mistake, not seen things clearly. That happens, Alfred thought, people are allowed to make mistakes. He always regretted that one simple decision though, and the thought of Rebecca limping off, alone, was to haunt him till his death.

In looking back, what came next seemed a constant whirl of new experiences. Alfred's whole life was divided into what happened before he passed through Seacity's gate, and what happened after, with, over time, the memories of what happened before becoming gradually more faded and unreal.

Harald took him into the city and put him in the care of a teacher he knew. Alfred must have pleased them in some way as he was soon taken up and educated in a merchant's guild; Harald maybe called in a favour, he had mused at the time, to get him into one of the most privileged bodies in the city. He was taught writing and reading, which he seemed to pick up with an ease that surprised everyone, and he spent his time navigating the endless twists and tunnels of Seacity with a delight that never left him.

It wasn't until several weeks had passed, rather than the days that he had promised, that he finally went out to see Rebecca. Why this was, why he waited so long, he could never really answer. He had been told where she was, of course, and Harald had given him updates to his questions. But there was something else. A dark awareness of something at the back of his mind, a looming future that he shirked away from and did not want to face.

The day came though, that Alfred walked out to a small house almost in the shadow of the city walls, albeit on the distant and hard to reach side. Rebecca, as Harald had assured him and arranged, had been taken in by a family, who seemed kindly enough, and was helping out on the flower beds that they raised for the city. Rebecca had always been very able with anything that grew. As Alfred approached, she raised herself from where she had been planting, and looked up at him with a smile.

They talked then for a while, but it became hesitant, strained. An awkwardness seemed to have fallen between them. He touched her hand for a moment, but she didn't respond. She talked of how she liked it, where she was, and how it was probably for the best. She listened with interest to Alfred.
"You'll do well, Alfred. I always knew that you would," she had said.

Over the months that followed, Alfred went to see her every once in a while. He was clad now in the red cloak that showed to all that he was a young Guild master. She was even allowed to come into the city once, granted some special dispensation, and expressed some wonder at the city but said, at the end of the day, that she was happy to go back to her home.

Alfred remembered the girl he had fell for around then. Rosaline with red hair and very pretty. In a whirl of passion and lust, he had feared losing her through her discovering his connection to Rebecca. Months went by without a visit to Rebecca till, one day, he had spied Rosaline holding hands with a young soldier.

The next day, he went out to Rebecca's small farm. The family were there but, to all his questions, they could only say that she had left. That she had met a young man who had heard of an opportunity further north.

Alfred left the house and looked up the road. He could see the fringe of the forest rising like a distant green wall.

X

Alfred fulfilled all the promise in him that Harald saw and more. Within a year, he was allowed into the inner chambers of the guild where learning, thought lost by the rest of the world, was still kept. In these dark inner chambers, whole rooms were given over to books – often incomplete, torn, burnt (it turned out that there were other things that the travellers looked for and brought back to Seacity). Not just books though, charts, diagrams, maps of the world as it had been before the fires of the last war. Once one had become a full member of the guild, one could, with the proper permissions, access these and proceed with the knowledge gained as one desired (though Alfred always suspected, and rightly it turned out, that there were still other hoards of the most valuable items that only a further select few could see).

Within another few years, Alfred was taken into the bowels of one of the keeps. There he saw strange 'mechanics' being constructed, some with the metal and plastic Alfred had seen in those sacks. There were mutterings of machines that could think, machines that could move.

This was not to be Alfred's world. He, it turned out, had other gifts. In his first flush of manhood he boarded a ship, clad in the green robe that identified him, bound for foreign lands. He made friends and allies. Influence followed, power and wealth not far behind.

Postscript

A man past the prime of his years gets out of the carriage. It is his privilege to be the first to make the ceremonial journey to this, the most distant of SeaCity's territories. A man of his status, he had the option to turn this largely ceremonial journey down, but other thoughts had tugged at him as he had lain in bed at night.

The carriage door opened, and he alighted. The blighted place he remembered was gone, replaced by a village of small means but no apparent distress. Being shown around the settlement, he noted the rebuilt walls, the newly dug gardens, the sound rooves, the swept floors. There was no one here, it seemed, who knew him

Funny, he thought, how the shadows that had lurked on the edge of his thoughts for so long, seemed suddenly so distant in this clean, spare, safe little place. Two children ran past him playing. An older person (his own age, he thought with some displeasure) sat outside in the sun.

They came to the last little house, set against the vast plains that stretched, as always, to the north, like a stone that the tide had left. A woman, disfigured in a way that was becoming a rare sight now, bent over the furrows tugging at something. She was silhouetted against the sun that was starting to set far to the west, so Alfred placed a hand on his eyes to see. The figure straightened up and looked at him.

Stay in the know - subscribe to our newsletter!
https://dimensionfold.com/join/